THE LiON AND THE BiRD

MARiANNE DUBUC

ENCHANTED LION BOOKS
NEW YORK

Lion is working in his garden
when he hears a sound.

Oh! Poor little thing!
Lion can't just leave him there.

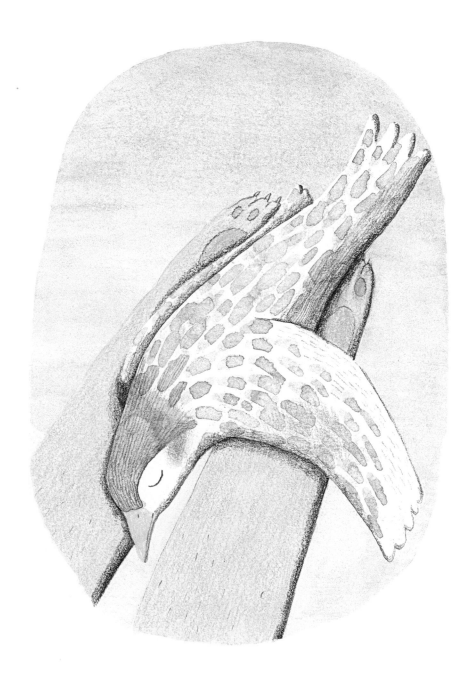

"Let's bandage you up," says Lion. "That will help."

"Oh no! They're flying away."

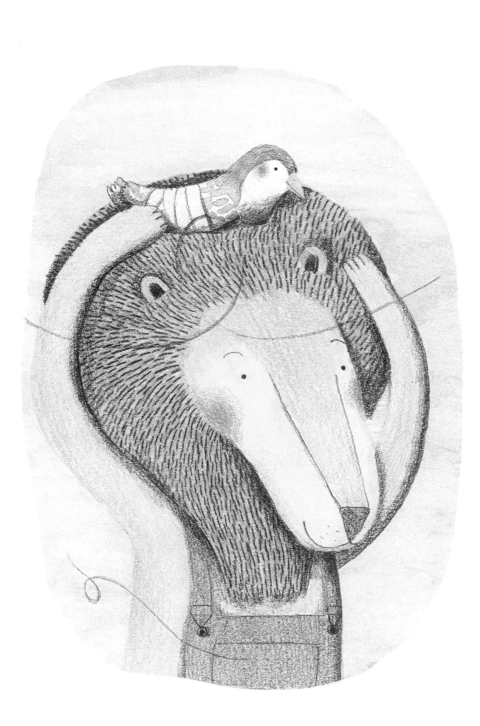

"Don't worry! You won't be cold here."

"You're welcome to stay with me.
There's more than enough room for both of us."

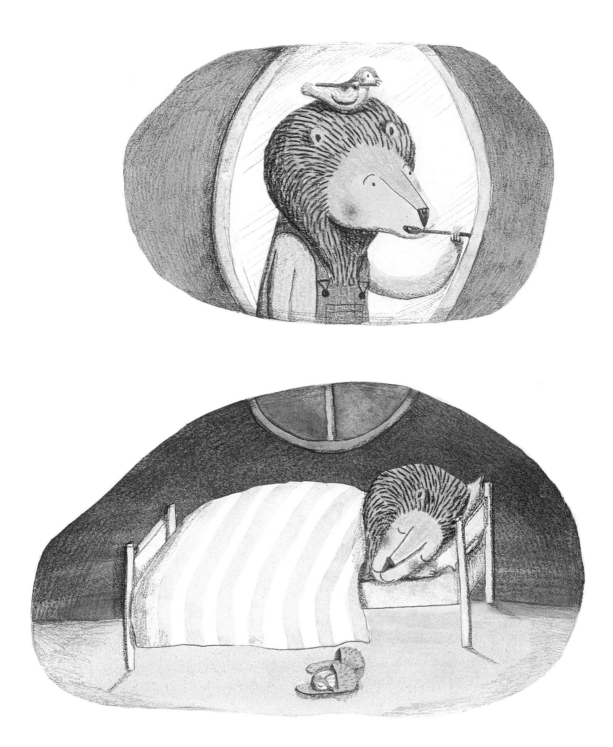

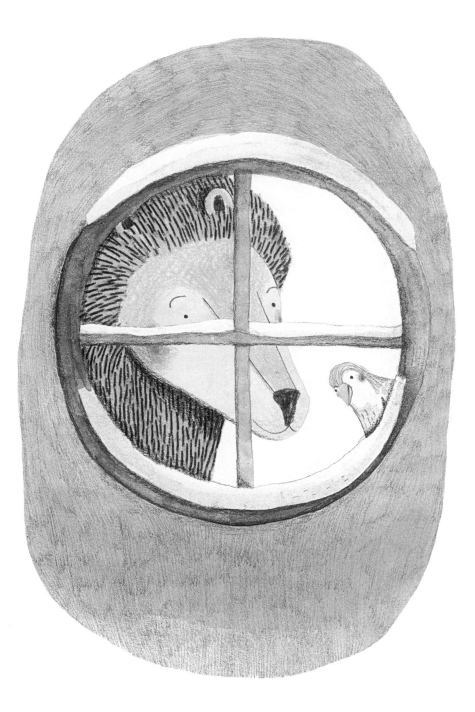

"Look, it's snowing."

"The snow is cold and icy, but you're snug and warm."

They spend the winter together, enjoying each day.

It snows and snows.

But winter doesn't feel all that cold with a friend.

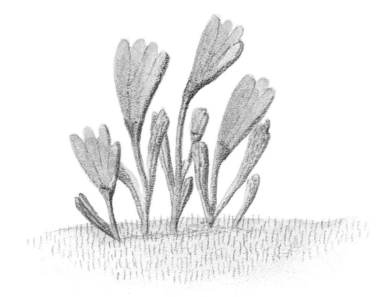

Then one day, spring returns.

And the others too.

"Yes," says Lion. "I know."

And so it goes.
Sometimes life is like that.

Lion's garden grows.

Summer passes slowly, softly.

Then one day, autumn returns.

And how about you? Lion wonders.

Maybe…

"Together, we'll stay warm again this winter."

JJ
DUBUC
MARIANNE

www.enchantedlionbooks.com

First American edition published in 2014 by Enchanted Lion Books, 351 Van Brunt Street, Brooklyn, NY 11231
English-language translation copyright © 2014 by Enchanted Lion Books
First published in French in 2013 by Les éditions de la Pastèque as *Le lion et l'oiseau*
Text and illustrations copyright © 2013 by Marianne Dubuc
Translated from the French by Claudia Z. Bedrick
All rights reserved under International and Pan-American Copyright Conventions
A CIP record is on file with the Library of Congress
ISBN: 978-1-59270-151-3. Printed in January 2014 by South China Printing Company